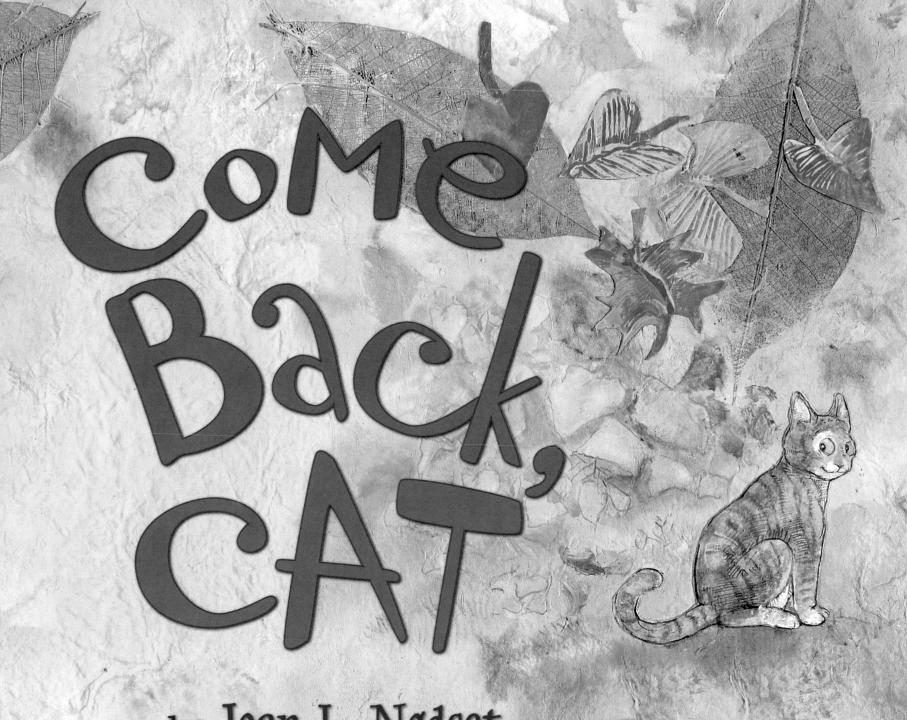

CoMe BaCk, CAT,

by Joan L. Nødset
pictures by
Steven Kellogg

For that Ptolemy Kayden, who started it all.
And with fond memories of my several successive
and each very special Amy Lou Lexau cats.
—J.L.N.

For dear Makena lei and her wonderful mom.
With love
—S.K.

Come here, cat.

Come here, you pretty cat.

You don't like me
to carry you that way?

I didn't mean to pull your tail.
You ran away when I was petting it.

Did I hurt you, cat?

I'll put you on my lap.
Stay here, now.
That's a good cat.

Yes, you can lick my face.
That feels funny.
Your tongue feels so rough.

Don't bite me, cat!
Don't, don't, don't!
Bad cat!

Oh, you were playing.
Well, you scared me, cat.
That's why I pushed you.

But it's okay now.

You can
come back,
cat.

Did I scare you too?
Look, I'll sit here,
nice and quiet.

That's it.

Just a little more.

I love you, cat!

Oh, cat!

I hear your motor.

Come Back, Cat
Text copyright © 1973, 2001 by Joan L. Nødset
Illustrations copyright © 2008 by Steven Kellogg

Manufactured in China.

Library of Congress Cataloging–in–Publication Data is available.
ISBN 978-0-06-028081-9 (trade bdg.) — ISBN 978-0-06-028082-6 (lib. bdg.)

Design by Stephanie Bart–Horvath
1 2 3 4 5 6 7 8 9 10
◆
Text originally published in 1973 by Harper & Row, New York, under the title Come Here, Cat